# The Cat with Seven Names

Tony Johnston

*Illustrated by* Christine Davenier

ini Charlesbridge

*For Regis, the noblest cat I have ever known.*
—T. J.

*For the Taylor family (Pascale, Steve, Laura, and Adrian);*
*so cool to be a cat in their house!*
—C. D.

Published by Charlesbridge
85 Main Street
Watertown, MA 02472
(617) 926-0329
www.charlesbridge.com

**Library of Congress Cataloging-in-Publication Data**
Johnston, Tony, 1942–
   The cat with seven names/Tony Johnston; illustrated by Christine Davenier.
      p. cm.
Summary: A wandering cat brightens the lives of six lonely people—and
persuades all of them to feed him until a near accident brings them all together.
   ISBN 978-1-58089-381-7 (reinforced for library use)
   ISBN 978-1-60734-602-9 (ebook)
1. Cats—Juvenile fiction. 2. Loneliness—Juvenile fiction. [1. Cats—Fiction.
2. Loneliness—Fiction.] I. Davenier, Christine, ill. II. Title.

PZ7.J6478Cat 2013
813.54—dc23      2012024434

Printed in Singapore
(hc) 10 9 8 7 6 5 4 3 2 1

Illustrations done in ink and colored pencils on Keaykolour paper
Display type set in Pablo by Esselte Letraset Ltd.
Text type set in Schneidler BT by Bitstream, Inc.
Color separations by KHL Chroma Graphics, Singapore
Printed in February 2013 by Imago in Singapore
Production supervision by Brian G. Walker
Designed by Diane M. Earley

**A cat came** to my back door one day. Gray, with white paws. Nobody visits me much. I put down the book I was reading (I am a librarian), and I let him in.

I figured he was a stray, so I fed him. Tuna.

He purred like he was motorized, as if thanking me for the delightful fish. Then he wandered off to "check out" my house. That's librarian humor.

After half an hour, I found my visitor. Napping on a bookshelf. I told him, "Since you enjoy books, you can stay." Now he comes here often. We read together. The big feline is partial to books involving cats and fish. Books like *Jenny and the Cat Club, The Old Man and the Sea,* and *A River Runs Through It.* He is so big I have dubbed him Stuart Little.

**I went out** for the paper once, in the cold of dawn. Left the door ajar. With my walker I moved slow as molasses. So a cat slipped in. Just like that. My family's grown and gone, so this small bit of company felt nice. Kinda filled up the house again.

Cat moved softly through my place, like a trail of
smoke, nimbly avoiding the walker (though he paused to
sniff my boots). 'Course, unlike smoke he spoke the whole
time, in cat talk. How good to hear a voice other than the
blab of my own. Cat talked so earnest, I felt certain he
must be starved, though his full figure told otherwise.

In any case, his cries turned my heart to butter. So I gave him a nibble from last night's supper.

"No offense," I whispered. "It's catfish."

No offense taken. Reg'lar as clockwork my friend
comes back.
Name's Kitty-boy. I hope he likes that.

**One afternoon** *una tormenta,* a storm, came.
It rained *gatos y perros.* Especially *gatos.* I imagine
that is why that big gray *gato* turned up at *mi
casa.* He poured down from the *cielo,* the sky.

I heard him before I saw him. Big singing *voz,*
even in a storm. Like Placido Domingo, *mi favorito.*

Since *mi señora* passed on—*mi tesoro,* my
treasure—I am pretty alone, with only *mi perro,*
my dog. This neighborhood, it is good. But here
people are busy, busy. They move quick, quick.
Like *grillos,* crickets, hopping here and everywhere.
For friendships, they have little time.

In spite of *mi perro,* I took this sopping *gato* in,
toweled him off and fed him part of a taco. That one,
he gobbled it up. For certain he is *Mexicano.*

"Placido," I said, "you keep dry, *amigo,* to stay in
good *voz."* Then for him I fixed up the doghouse.
(It was only for looks, anyhow. On my bed,
that is where *mi perro* sleeps.)

That Placido keeps in good *voz* all right. He comes and sings arias to me *diario,* each day.

**"Move it,** you big lump. I'm on duty," I said.
(Cold day, warm engine. The cat was no dummy.)

The cat yawned, mouth wide like the MGM lion.
He threaded through my legs. Got fur on my
uniform. I didn't mind. My hours are long.
Not much chance to chew the fat with anyone.

When he saw my lunch, he gave it a green-eyed
stare. A cat that size *couldn't* be hungry. Still, as an
officer of the law, I try to give everybody the benefit
of the doubt. So I gave him a bite of my Big Mac.
I called him Mooch after that.

Sometimes when I'm on patrol I see him, and I stop to converse. He flops himself in my path to be petted, and he bats those big green eyes and purrs like a Cadillac. I laugh—and I pet him. Once he hopped into my vehicle. "Gonna have to ticket you, Mooch," I said. But I didn't give him a ticket. I gave him some more burger instead.

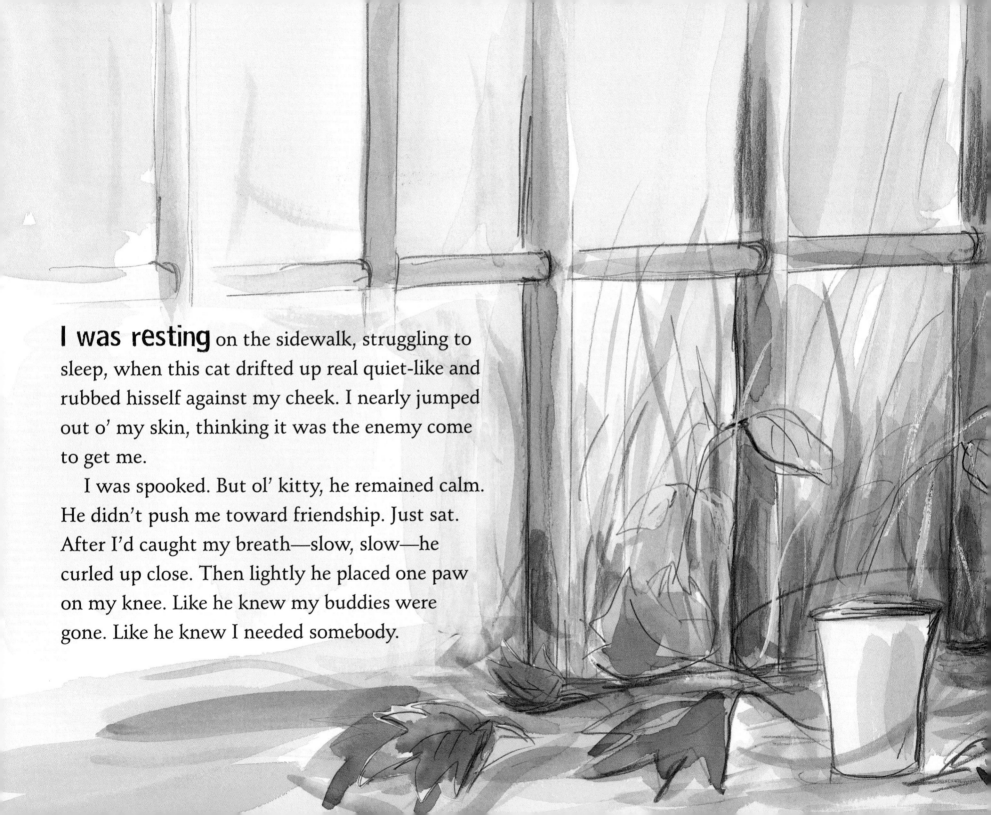

**I was resting** on the sidewalk, struggling to sleep, when this cat drifted up real quiet-like and rubbed hisself against my cheek. I nearly jumped out o' my skin, thinking it was the enemy come to get me.

I was spooked. But ol' kitty, he remained calm. He didn't push me toward friendship. Just sat. After I'd caught my breath—slow, slow—he curled up close. Then lightly he placed one paw on my knee. Like he knew my buddies were gone. Like he knew I needed somebody.

I can't feed him anything. Can't feed my own self most of the time. Ol' kitty, he seems to know that and doesn't beg.

Once I was in a war, so now everything makes me jumpy. Good days, I can push horrors away some. Bad days, my mind recalls the terrible sounds. But on cat days, well, I smile. Truly. And I sleep. Ol' kitty brings me comfort and silence—and a speck of peace.

That's why I call him Dove.

"Mom! Mom! There's a cat on the roof!"
I called. And—*poof!*—like magic, suddenly the cat
was beside me. With a whole throat full of purrs.
  "Isn't he beautiful, Mom?"
Mom said he was.
  "Isn't he sweet, Mom?"
Mom said he was.

"He's hungry, Mom."

Mom said he wasn't. She said the cat had overindulged—he was absolutely *obese*.

"Can I feed him, Mom?"

Mom said I couldn't.

Mom and I were new to this place, and we didn't know anyone yet. I just *knew* we needed this cat.

"Please," I begged. "Please, please, *please,* with pretty sugar on top?" I made my eyes big. Like the cat's.

Mom said okay, but not to give him anything fancy.

"Here, Mouse," I said, "have some leftover ham."

Now Mouse visits a lot. While he's eating I tell him stories, mostly about other cats. Mouse seems to like the stories. But sometimes he falls asleep and snores.